D1180790

When Barbie was asked to model the Dream Glow Collection for her friends Tim and Sue, she was pleased. No one realised that mischief was afoot – a rival designer was so jealous that he was determined to ruin the show. He might have succeeded but for some quick thinking...

British Library Cataloguing in Publication Data
Cameron, Joan
The Dream Glow collection.—(Barbie; 1)
I. Title II. Raymond, Kim III. Series
823'.914[J] PZ7
ISBN 0-7214-0990-3

First edition

Published by Ladybird Books Ltd Loughborough Leicestershire UK
Ladybird Books Inc Lewiston Maine 04240 USA

© LADYBIRD BOOKS LTD MCMLXXXVI and MATTEL INC MCMLXXXVI
Barbie and associated characters are US trademarks of, and used under licence from, Mattel Inc. All rights reserved. No part of this publication may be reproduced, stored in a retrieval system, or transmitted in any form or by any means, electronic, mechanical, photo-copying, recording or otherwise, without the prior consent of the copyright owners.

Printed in England

The Dream Glow Collection

by JOAN CAMERON
illustrated by KIM RAYMOND

Ladybird Books

One bright morning, Barbie visited Sue, an old school friend. Sue and her twin brother, Tim, were successful fashion designers. Together, they had founded their own fashion house, and "Timsu Designs" had become well known all over the world. Barbie loved their clothes, and often wore them herself.

Sue brought out a folder of fashion drawings. As Barbie watched, she laid them out on the table. Barbie looked from one drawing to another. Each design seemed more exciting than the one before.

"They're lovely!" Barbie cried. "They're the best you've ever done!"

Sue smiled happily.

"I'm pleased you like them, Barbie," she said. "You see, these are the drawings for our next Spring Collection. We're using special material that glows in the dark, so we've called the Collection 'Dream Glow'. It's to be seen for the first time at a big Spring Fashion Show in Paris. We'd like you to model the dresses for us."

Barbie gave her friend a quick hug.

"I'd love to," she said simply.

Work on the "Dream Glow" Collection went on all winter. Timsu Designs had workshops and an elegant Salon in London's Mayfair. Every now and then Barbie had fittings there. Her boyfriend, Ken, usually went with her, but if he was away, Barbie's sister, Skipper, took his place.

On one of Skipper's visits, Barbie's poodle, Prince, went along too. Barbie led the way into the Salon.

"I hope you won't be bored, Skipper," she said, handing her coat to one of the receptionists, a dark-haired girl called Maria. "I'll be quite some time in the fitting rooms."

"Don't worry," Skipper told her. "I love it here. And I'll take Prince for a walk later."

For a time, Skipper sat watching people bustling to and fro in the busy Salon. But soon Prince tugged at his lead, and looked up appealingly.

"All right, Prince," Skipper laughed. "We'll go for that walk now."

The fashion house overlooked a wide square. The gardens in the centre were filled with trees and bushes. As she walked along, Skipper noticed a girl hurrying through the trees ahead of them. She had her coat collar turned up, hiding her face.

"How odd," thought Skipper.

Next moment, the girl had gone.

Skipper and Prince strolled round the square, enjoying the winter sun. When the Timsu Salon was out of sight behind the trees, Skipper saw the mystery girl again. This time she was half-hidden in a doorway. She was talking furtively to an older man with black hair and a neat, pointed beard.

Skipper frowned. "I think she works at the Timsu Salon," she murmured to herself.

But she wasn't certain. And before she was near enough to be sure, the girl saw her. She darted away, still keeping her face hidden. The man

brushed past Skipper, giving her an angry look before he, too, hurried away. The look was so angry that Prince growled, deep in his throat.

Skipper stood still for a moment, puzzled.

"Well! Did we interrupt a secret meeting or something?" she wondered aloud.

Just then, Prince spotted a cat. Barking furiously, he tried to give chase. By the time she had calmed the dog down, Skipper had forgotten all about the mystery girl.

Spring came, and at last the Fashion Show was only hours away. Barbie, Skipper and Ken had flown to Paris to help Sue and Tim with last-minute preparations.

They were all excited about the Show. It was the most colourful event of the fashion year. Fashion writers and buyers from all over the world would be there.

The "Dream Glow" Collection was ready. The designs were top secret, and no one was to see them until the Show itself. To keep them hidden each dress, newly pressed, was inside its own special, sealed bag. Nothing could be seen of what was inside. Each bag was hung neatly on racks, inside a store-room at the hotel where the friends were staying.

Once the last bag was in its place, Tim locked the store-room door.

"All ready," he said, with a cheerful grin.

Barbie took Sue's arm.

"Let's go out for a walk," she suggested. "You've worked hard all day, Sue. You need a break."

The evening was warm, and the lights of Paris twinkled brightly in the dusk. People were everywhere, strolling through the parks and along the boulevards. The soft air was filled with the murmur of their voices and the roar of the traffic streaming past.

Ken took Barbie's hand as they walked. Barbie sighed happily. She loved Paris, especially in springtime, when dreary winter days were forgotten.

Skipper suddenly stopped dead, pointing to a man who'd just come out of a pavement café.

"I've seen that man before!" she exclaimed.

Sue gasped, and drew back. "That's Ivan Lisse – I hope he doesn't see us!"

She need not have worried. The man stood at the edge of the pavement, his back towards them. He seemed to be waiting for someone.

"Who is he?" Barbie asked, wondering why Sue seemed so upset.

Tim explained. Ivan Lisse was another designer, well known in the fashion world for many years. However, the Timsu clothes were far more popular than his had ever been, and he'd become very jealous.

"He has even tried to buy our designs," Tim went on. "He hates the idea of having to compete with a Timsu Collection at the Show tomorrow."

Skipper told them when and where she had seen Ivan Lisse, and with whom.

"I think he was talking to Maria, one of your receptionists," she said, "but I was really too far away to be sure. She certainly didn't seem to want me to see her."

Sue clutched Tim's arm. "Maria has been asking too many questions lately! Tim – what if she's given Lisse copies of our designs?"

"She can't have, Sue." Tim shook his head firmly. "You know that the designs are kept locked up. The only people who ever see them – or the dresses – are the cutting and sewing room staff. And we've always trusted them completely, haven't we?"

"He might try to steal the dresses from the hotel," Sue said, anxiously.

Tim patted his sister's hand. "Stop worrying, Sue! Look – he's meeting friends, and they're driving away."

As they watched, a car drew up, with two men inside. Ivan Lisse got in, and the car moved off. It was soon lost in the traffic. Sue said no more, but Barbie could see her friend was troubled.

The friends walked slowly back to their hotel. Skipper went unwillingly to bed, and the others stood on the balcony outside their suite of rooms, chatting. Barbie could see that Sue was still worried. She touched Ken's arm.

"Ken, I think I know how we can set Sue's mind at rest," she murmured.

They talked quietly together for a moment or two, then Barbie explained her plan to Sue and Tim. Ken was going to stay up all night, outside the room where the dresses were kept. He'd keep guard, while the others went to bed. They'd need their sleep for the Show next day...

Midnight found Ken settled in a chair outside the store-room. It was to be a long weary night for him. He read, but as it grew later and later, he found his eyes closing over his book. Every now and then he stood up and stretched, to keep himself awake. All the time, unknown to him, someone was watching, waiting for him to fall asleep.

But Ken stayed awake. Four o'clock, five o'clock – would this night ever end? It was almost six when the hotel night porter hurried along the corridor towards him.

"Please come downstairs, m'sieu," he said. "There is an urgent telephone call for you."

Ken cast a quick glance at the store-room door. Surely no one would come now? He nodded to the porter. "I'll come."

As soon as Ken and the porter were out of sight, two men appeared from the fire escape. With them – Maria, the girl from the Timsu Salon! One of the men had a pass-key, and he swiftly opened the store-room door.

"Hurry!" hissed Maria. "Before he comes back!"

Quickly, the three of them took all the security bags from the racks and carried them to the waiting service elevator. The doors closed. The elevator dropped swiftly to the basement – and the furnace room.

Ivan Lisse was waiting there, his eyes gleaming with triumph.

"Throw the dresses in the furnace!" he ordered.

One by one, the Timsu security bags were thrown into the flames. Soon they were burning fiercely.

"They'll never make new dresses in time!" Lisse crowed, clapping his hands in delight. "*My* dresses will be the highlight of the Show!"

Meanwhile, down in the hotel lobby, the night porter handed Ken the telephone receiver. Ken put it to his ear, but the line was silent.

"Hello?" Ken listened, then shook his head. "There's no one there!"

"I am sorry, m'sieu," the porter spread out his hands. "The lady said it was most urgent. She even told me where to find you."

Ken's lips twitched. The call had been a trick to lure him away from the store-room! The porter watched in surprise as Ken raced for the stairs, and took them two at a time.

Ken found the door to the store-room wide open. Grimly, he looked inside. The racks were empty.

Just then, Skipper appeared at his side. She'd wakened very early. Too excited to go back to sleep, she had come to see Ken. She caught sight of the empty racks, and Ken's face.

"Oh, no!" she wailed. "The dresses have gone!"

* * *

The Fashion Show was staged in one of the biggest hotels in Paris. The salon was crowded, the men in smart suits, the women glittering with diamonds. Sue and Tim were there, too, standing quietly near the door.

As they stood there, Ivan Lisse came in, and Maria was with him. Lisse couldn't resist sneering at them.

"Is your Collection ready?" he taunted.

Just then, the lights in the vast room dimmed. The Show was about to begin! The room grew quiet as the audience settled down. Men in scarlet and white uniforms stepped forward, and stood in a row under a spotlight. Raising silver trumpets to their lips, they sounded a rousing fanfare. The last notes died away, and there was complete silence.

It only lasted a second. Then the room was in darkness, except for a glittering curtain on the stage. Barbie suddenly appeared through it.

She was wearing the first of the Dream Glow dresses, and it really did glow in the dark. As she

danced along the catwalk, her dress shimmered in folds from her blonde hair to the tips of her golden sandals.

The audience gasped. Someone murmured: "Isn't she lovely?"

Barbie modelled dress after dress, and the audience became more and more excited.

For the finale, Barbie wore the most glamorous gown from the Collection, and she seemed to float across the stage in a cloud of glowing colour. Ken came on as her escort, in a jacket and trousers that sparkled under the lights. The audience burst into a storm of applause.

Sue and Tim hugged one another in delight. The audience was still applauding. The Dream Glow Collection was even more successful than the twins had hoped.

Ivan Lisse stared, his mouth open. He couldn't understand it – he'd burnt the Dream Glow Collection – but here it was, and everyone loved it. Behind him, Maria's face had turned white.

"Thought you'd taken our Collection, didn't you!" Tim spoke very softly to the other man. "Well, you didn't, thanks to Barbie!"

Ivan Lisse didn't answer. He glared at Tim, then stalked out of the room, pushing Maria out of his way as he went.

"Looks as if she isn't working for Ivan Lisse any more," Tim said.

"– Or for us!" Sue added.

Then she smiled, and the two of them went forward to join Barbie and Ken on stage. The audience cheered them to the echo.

Later, over lunch, as they were celebrating the success of the "Dream Glow" Collection, Skipper suddenly looked cross. "Will someone please tell me what happened after I went to bed last night?" she asked. "Everyone's been too busy to explain!"

Sue laughed. "Barbie made a great suggestion, and saved the Collection," she told Skipper. "Last night, we took the dresses out of their security bags, and hung them up in our bedrooms. They took up a lot of room, but it was worth it!"

"Barbie was afraid Maria might have told Lisse

where we were staying, and that he might try to steal the dresses," Ken chimed in. "As it turned out, she was right."

Skipper still looked puzzled.

"But what *did* he steal? Empty bags?"

"Oh, no." Barbie took up the story. "The bags weren't empty. We put something into them, to make it look as if there were dresses inside."

She paused, her eyes twinkling, then went on: "Ivan Lisse stole a Collection of old hotel bed sheets!"